MW00905792

Tent Show

DISCARD

CHILI PUBLIC LIBRARY

MAR 2 6 '91

Tent Show

by Susan Saunders

illustrated by Diane Allison

DUTTON CHILDREN'S BOOKS
NEW YORK

Text copyright © 1990 by Susan Saunders
Illustrations copyright © 1990 by Diane Allison

All rights reserved. No part of this publication may be
reproduced or transmitted in any form or by any means,
electronic or mechanical, including photocopy, recording,
or any information storage and retrieval system now
known or to be invented, without permission in writing
from the publisher, except by a reviewer who wishes to
quote brief passages in connection with a review written
for inclusion in a magazine, newspaper, or broadcast.

Library of Congress Cataloging-in-Publication Data

Saunders, Susan.
    Tent show / by Susan Saunders; illustrated by Diane Allison—
1st ed.
        p. cm.
    Summary: One memorable summer afternoon in a small
town, a girl who is disgusted that her older sister is marrying
and settling down listens to a story told by a contemporary
of her grandmother, and from that moment on views life a
little differently.
    ISBN 0-525-44598-6
    I. Allison, Diane Worfolk, ill. II. Title.
PZ7.S2577Te 1990   89-38565
[Fic]—dc20   CIP
                                                          AC

Published in the United States by
Dutton Children's Books,
a division of Penguin Books USA Inc.

Published simultaneously in Canada by
Fitzhenry & Whiteside Limited, Toronto

Printed in the U.S.A.   First Edition
10 9 8 7 6 5 4 3 2 1

to Honor and Catherine Keeler

S.S.

to Mom

D.A.

Contents

The Cypress Tree

"I'm not going to Mrs. Dowe's to try on that dumb dress! And I'm not going to be in the dumb wedding!"

"Ellie!"

Ellie flung open the screen door.

"You get back in here this minute, young lady!" her mother said firmly. But Ellie had already flounced down the kitchen steps and was stalking across the backyard.

A small black-and-white dog raised his head from the damp earth under the oleander bush. He cocked an ear at Ellie. Then he scrambled to his feet, shaking the dirt off his wiry fur.

"Just stay out of my way, Shorty!" Ellie muttered as she stomped past him.

Shorty fell into line behind her, trotting at Ellie's heels until she halted at the base of the cypress tree. When she reached for the knotted rope hanging from its lowest branch, the dog sat down. He scratched his ribs thoughtfully, keeping an eye on his owner.

The cypress was old, one of the oldest trees in town. Like the cedars on Main Street, it was an evergreen, with evenly spaced branches that grew shorter as they marched up its scaly gray trunk. But it was three times the size of a cedar, too thick at the bottom for Ellie to stretch her arms around.

Ellie's Great-aunt Jane had dug the cypress up on a trip to the Neches River when she was a little girl. "It won't grow here. It's too dry," everybody had told Jane.

But she watered the little cypress through many hot summers, until its roots reached

down to the underground stream that ran far
under Caldwell and never dried up.

There was nothing Aunt Jane could do
about the wind, though. It blew into town
from the southeast most of the time, stirring
up a pink haze of dust. The cypress would
have been fifty feet tall if it had grown
straight. Over the years the wind had bent
the tree until it looked as though it was bow-
ing from the waist, toward Ellie's house.

As Ellie stood in its shade, her hand on the rope, undecided, a car rumbled around the corner. It edged up to the curb in front of her house. Car doors opened and closed.

"Ellie?" her mother called from inside the kitchen. "Your grandmother is here to take us to Mrs. Dowe's!"

"No! Not if I have to stay right in this tree till the buzzards get me!" Ellie exclaimed fiercely.

She grabbed the rope with both hands and pulled herself up the crooked trunk. Ellie straddled the lowest branch just long enough to take a deep breath of the piney smell of cypress. Then she climbed all the way up to the tip of the tree.

There she sat down, her legs dangling. The tree swayed gently as the wind blew cool against her warm face.

Her mother had stopped calling her. Now Ellie could hear new voices. One of them belonged to her grandmother: "Where is that child?" But Ellie wasn't sure about the other one. If she twisted around and leaned forward just a little . . . Three women were peering out at the cypress through the screen door! Her mother, and Grandma Catherine—but Ellie didn't think she'd ever seen the third woman before. She wasn't wearing a pants suit, like the other ladies in Caldwell, or a skirt and blouse. She had on a flimsy, flowing dress and wore her gray hair long, and there were big yellow beads around her neck.

Weird! Ellie said to herself.

Ellie's mother was speaking softly, but Ellie could make out words here and there: " . . . bridesmaid . . . only four weeks . . . fitting. . . . " Was she going to tell the strange woman *everything*?

Ellie sucked in some air, threw her head back—and howled, like Mrs. Jennings' beagle at the end of the block. If she did it just right, half the dogs in town would answer her, starting with the Culvers' bird dog, Skipper. Ellie howled again.

Yes, there was Skipper, starting out low and rising to a shriek. In a few seconds, the beagle down the street, Chico, joined in with a mellow *o-o-o-o*.

Pat and Mike, the two brown dogs across the alley, raised their voices in a shrill duet. Then Shorty added a chorus of yelps.

Ellie grinned. Once she'd gotten them going, they'd keep it up for a while, making enough noise to drown out her mother, and ten or twelve other people besides. She settled back against a spray of soft needles to think.

From her perch in the cypress, Ellie had the whole dusty town spread out in front of her: the square cream-colored courthouse, the sign on the front of the Majestic Movie Theater, the scalloped roof of the White Wing Hotel. She could look clear across Caldwell in every direction. But what could she really see? Certainly nothing worth seeing, as far as she was concerned!

"And Mary Beth wants to stay here forever?" Ellie groaned and closed her eyes.

As the tree swayed up and down, she imagined herself in a sailboat, rocking on the swells of an ocean. She was the youngest girl to cross the Atlantic alone. A storm howled around her ship. She'd lashed herself to the mast, and . . .

Over the racket of the dogs, Ellie heard car doors slamming shut. She opened her eyes. Shorty stopped yipping to listen. And Grandma Catherine's car grumbled to life and rattled away, up the street.

"They've gone without me." Ellie nodded, satisfied. "Mama knows I mean what I say."

The howls of Pat and Mike across the alley were weakening. The beagle didn't hold out much longer, either. And finally Skipper stopped, except for a whine now and then.

That's when someone spoke, almost directly beneath the cypress tree.

"Well, this is a lovely thing to happen!

And look at the gazebo! It'll cost forty
pounds to mend it. People have no right to
do such things!"

Ellie stared down between her feet. It was
the strange old lady. She was talking to herself—not in a low voice, the way Ellie did,
but *loud*!

Sara

The old lady laughed unpleasantly. "What sort of woman is that to have as a guest, when you know all of Tewkesbury will be calling on us to see the aeroplane?"

What she was saying didn't make any sense, and she talked funny, too. Ellie inched carefully down the cypress tree to get a clearer look at the stranger.

The old lady was bending over, speaking directly to Shorty. "Bunny, come with me and help me to get all the people out of the grounds. I declare, they came running as if they'd sprung out of the earth."

" 'Bunny?' Anybody can see he's a dog,"

Ellie mumbled. "I believe Mama's gone off and left me with a crazy person!"

Shorty didn't seem to mind what the old lady called him. He wagged his stump of a tail and smiled at her, showing the row of tiny teeth in the front of his mouth.

Ellie had leaned so far out of the tree by then that one of her feet slipped. She grabbed a branch to steady herself, and tore a chunk of gray bark loose. It fell to the ground beside the woman's shoe.

The woman straightened up slowly and gazed into the cypress. Clear green eyes met Ellie's brown ones. She doesn't really look crazy, Ellie decided.

"Hello," the stranger said. "You're Ellie, aren't you? My name is Sara Forster."

"Hello," Ellie replied cautiously.

Sara fanned herself with a book she was holding. "Whew!" she said. "I'd forgotten how hot it is down here in the summertime."

"Where do you live?" Ellie asked her.

"New York City," Sara answered.

"Oh." New York City—no wonder she acts so peculiar. Ellie climbed down another branch. "How do you know us, then?"

"Your grandmother and I were in elementary school together," Sara replied. "Until my family moved down the road to Dillard, Catherine and I were best friends."

Ellie knew what her grandmother had looked like as a little girl. There was a picture of her in the upstairs hall. But when she tried to imagine her Grandma Catherine and this lady playing together, she couldn't.

Sara fanned herself again, and sank down onto a white lawn chair. "They tell me your sister's getting married next month."

Ellie made a terrible face.

"You aren't happy about it?" Sara asked.

"Mary Beth planned on being a famous writer!" Ellie said indignantly. "She was going to graduate from the university and get a job in Houston—or maybe Dallas. And she said I could stay with her whenever I wanted."

· 12 ·

Sara nodded, listening.

"Now she's not even finishing college!" Ellie shook her head, disgusted. "She's marrying Mike Horton. They're going to live right here in Caldwell and raise hogs, like Mike's dad. The wedding's in four weeks, and . . . and I'm not coming down from this tree till it's over!"

Sara shaded her eyes against the sun with her hand. "Mary Beth can live in Caldwell and still be a writer, can't she?"

"But I know she won't!" Ellie said gloomily. "Why doesn't she want to *do* things?"

"Do you know what you want to do when you grow up?" Sara asked.

Ellie looked out over the town and shrugged her shoulders. "Be a stunt woman," she said. "Or make up songs and sell them for a million dollars. Fly to Mars. I don't know—I'm only nine years and four months old," Ellie pointed out.

"Nine years and four months. When I was

about your age, I knew there was another world out there, too, where people led all kinds of interesting lives." Sara smiled, remembering. "I just didn't know how to get to it. Then the tent show came to town."

"What's a tent show?" Ellie asked her.

"A tent show was a traveling theater," Sara answered. "We didn't have television, of course. Caldwell was even too small for movies in those days. So seeing real actors was thrilling. And I almost missed them."

"Why?" Ellie rested her elbows on a cypress limb.

"I didn't like my sister's boyfriend, Kyle, very much to begin with," Sara said. "And I'd gotten into big trouble because of him."

"What kind of trouble?" Ellie asked, interested.

"Well, Kyle could be kind of stuffy," Sara said. "He had a gray horse he called Lucky. . . . Do you want me to tell you about it?"

Sara's Story:
The Indian Horse

I was nine years old that summer. I thought Kyle's horse looked just like the horse the chief rode in my book about Indians. At least, Lucky *could* have looked like the chief's horse. He was the right color, a gleaming steel gray. All he needed was a red circle around his eye, and feathers in his mane and tail, and he'd be the horse the bravest chief would ride.

Kyle was very proud of Lucky. On Saturday afternoons, he'd brush him until his gray coat shone. Then Kyle would hitch Lucky to his parents' buggy and trot him over to our house to see Frances, my sister.

Kyle would tie the horse up in the shade of our cedar hedge. He'd go sit on the front porch with my mother and father. They'd drink lemonade and visit while Frances got ready to go for a ride in the buggy.

"Kyle's so stuck on himself!" I said to my mother once. "What does Frances want him around for?"

"He's a nice young man, Sara," my mother replied gently.

But I thought Kyle was conceited, and he thought I was a grubby little pest. We didn't like each other one bit. I usually stayed in my hideout in the cedar hedge with my dog until Kyle and Frances left for their buggy ride. My dog's name was Snip, and he was part Airedale and part bloodhound.

On this one Saturday afternoon, Snip and I were in the hedge, as usual. Snip was lying on his back in a hole he'd dug, sound asleep. I was watching Lucky stamp his feet and twitch his tail at flies—he had a beautiful dark gray tail streaked with silver—when

suddenly I had a great idea! Why not fix Lucky up like the chief's horse?

I scrambled out of the hedge and headed for the chicken pen. The ground inside the pen was always littered with feathers—speckled brown ones, black ones, gray-and-whites. It was Buster's feathers I had in mind, though, and he hadn't shed a single one.

Buster was our rooster. He had glossy green tail feathers that arched over until they swept the ground. I thought I'd hem him up in a corner and snatch a few. But Buster wouldn't be hemmed. As soon as I'd take a step toward him, Buster would strut in the opposite direction, with all his hens squawking nervously after him.

I tried running him down. But Buster was faster than I was, and he could fly a little, too. He fluttered away from me to perch on the edge of the chicken-house roof, where he cocked his head and studied me with a beady black eye.

"You're not as smart as you think you are," I said to him. I held out a cupped hand. "Chick, chick, chick," I called softly. "He-e-ere, chick, chick, chick." I shook my hand from side to side, the way we did when we scattered feed for the chickens.

The silly hens dashed forward to scratch at the ground near my feet. Buster clucked sus-

piciously, but he was too greedy to resist. He glided down from the roof of the chicken house.

I waited until he was just close enough. Then I threw myself on him! I heard my sash rip as I landed—girls didn't wear jeans when I was growing up—and Buster scratched my arm good. But I got four green feathers.

"Now all I need is some red paint," I said, dusting off the front of my dress.

I ended up with bluing from the wash-house instead. There was a big bottle of it sitting next to the tin washtubs. Mama poured just a little into the laundry to make the sheets whiter. In the bottle it was a nice dark blue color, just right to turn Lucky into an Indian horse.

I could hear Kyle holding forth on the porch to Frances and my parents—the coast was clear. I wove two feathers into the hair of Lucky's mane and fastened two more on-to his tail. Then I stuck my finger into the bottle of bluing. While Lucky blinked sleep-ily, I painted thick blue circles around both of his eyes. For the finishing touch, I poured more bluing onto my hand and pressed it against his shoulder. It left a streaky, dark blue handprint.

I was standing back, admiring my work, when Kyle and Frances started up the drive-way. I whirled around and hid my hand behind me, but Frances yelled: "Sara! Just look at you! Your dress is a sight!"

"What happened to you, honey?" My mother hurried toward me. "Your arms are all scratched! And what's wrong with your hand?"

But Kyle stared past me at Lucky, stamping his hooves in the shade. "I don't believe it!" Kyle bellowed, his face like thunder. "That kid has gone and painted my horse *blue*!"

Ellie grinned and moved farther down the tree. "Did you get a spanking?" she asked.

"No, my parents thought I was too old to spank," Sara answered. "To my mind, the punishment was a lot worse. Until the bluing on Lucky wore off, I had to go to bed at seven o'clock every night. I wasn't to leave the yard, either. And bluing is as strong as a dye.

"That's why I was sitting on the front porch with Frances, instead of roller-skating with your grandmother, when Charlie Green ran by."

"Mr. Green at the drugstore?" Ellie asked. The only Charlie Green she knew was a tall, thin man with white hair and a disapproving frown.

"He's the one," Sara said. "Charlie was so excited that he could hardly get the words out. 'Hurry!' he yelled. 'The tent show's in town!'"

CCCCCCCCCCCCCCCCCCCCCCCCC

Sara's Plan

I'd never seen a tent show, but if it was half as exciting as Charlie Green seemed to think it was . . . I jumped up from the front steps and ran into the house so fast that Snip was certain something dangerous was after me. "Mama, the tent show's here! Can I go see? Ple-e-ease— just for a minute," I begged over his barking.

"All right," my mother agreed at last. "But you have to come straight back. And take Frances with you, to keep you out of trouble."

"I'm not going anywhere with you until

you comb your hair." My sister turned up her nose. "It looks like the dog's been chewing on it." Frances was as fresh and neat as always, in a pale pink dress with lace around the neck.

I couldn't see what difference my hair made, but I didn't want to waste any time arguing—I dragged a comb through it. Then we set out for Main Street, with me hurrying Frances along.

Next to the courthouse was an open field where the men played ball on summer afternoons. By the time Frances and I got there, half the town was ahead of us, watching the tent going up.

I hardly knew where to look first: at a whole mob of trucks parked every whichway, with THE JAMES WEST PLAYERS painted in gold on their sides; at the men struggling with the hundreds of yards of brown tent canvas that billowed in the wind; at the show band members tuning up their instruments. Or, best of all, at the actors strolling toward the White Wing Hotel. I'd never seen such remarkable people!

A young woman in a yellow silk dress tugged at a Pekingese on a ribbon leash. Another woman wore a purple hat on her bright red hair, and she had ermines draped around her shoulders. An older man with a thick mustache and dark eyebrows—it was Mr. West himself—carried a big green parrot in a cage. As they walked up Main Street, the actors laughed and talked noisily, as if they were completely unaware of the crowd that was following them.

They looked different, they sounded different—visitors from the world outside! I wanted to get as close to them as I could. I was just about to squeeze between old Mrs. Larkin and her plump husband when I heard a deep voice say hello to the "pretty young lady in the pink dress."

A handsome actor made a low bow. He

handed my sister a rosebud from a button-
hole of his striped vest. Then he bowed to
me, too, and introduced himself to both of
us.

"I'm George McIntyre," he said in a rich,
warm baritone. "I hope to see both you ladies in the front row tonight."

Frances blushed and smiled, showing the
dimple in her cheek. But I looked down at
my left hand. It was still dyed blue, even
though I'd washed it a hundred times. I
knew there wasn't a chance Lucky's circles
had worn off, either. Unless my parents suddenly changed their minds, I wouldn't be in

the front row at the tent show that night. I wouldn't be going to the tent show at all.

But it wouldn't hurt to try. I started on my mother as soon as Frances and I got home. Finally she gave in a little: "We'll see what your father says."

She didn't sound hopeful though. And Daddy stood firm. "I'm afraid not," he said, examining my hand at suppertime. "I'm sorry, Sara, but blue is blue. You have to be in bed by seven o'clock."

And that's where I was, lying in bed upstairs with my light off, while Frances got
ready to go to the tent show. The door to my
room was open a crack, and I could see her
walking up and down the hall in her favorite
green dress.

Mr. West's musicians were playing in front
of the courthouse, waltzes and fox-trots and
marching tunes that drifted invitingly through
my bedroom window. I don't think I could
have stood it . . . if I hadn't had a plan.

"What kind of plan?" Ellie asked, stretch-
ing out on a limb and watching Sara's face.

"I was going to that tent show, or pop,"
Sara answered, scratching Shorty's chin with
the toe of her shoe.

I waited until Frances left with her friends,
and my mother came up to say good night.
"I know how disappointed you are," she told
me. "The tent show will be here for five
days. Maybe we can talk your daddy into

taking you before it leaves." She kissed my cheek. "I don't want Frances to wake you up when she gets home," Mama said, closing the bedroom door behind her.

I counted to two hundred in the dark, giving her plenty of time to get downstairs and safely settled again, in the living room with my father. Then I threw back the covers, hopped out of bed, and pulled off my nightgown. Under it I was wearing a shirt and a pair of overalls my Uncle John, a farmer, had given me. I even had my shoes on already.

I stuffed my pillow into the nightgown and smoothed the covers back over them. I laid a sleeve of the gown across the top sheet, to make it look more like me, sleeping. Then I climbed over the windowsill and into the hackberry tree next to the house.

Sara Goes to the Tent Show

I'd spent a lot of time in that hackberry, but I'd always climbed it from the bottom up. Starting at the top felt kind of funny to me. I worked my way down the branches as quickly and quietly as I could.

As I slid the rest of the way to the ground, I saw my parents sitting in the living room. They were reading the newspaper, with Snip asleep on the floor between them. Mama and Daddy were probably the only people in Caldwell who'd stayed at home that night. They had to, because of me, and I was leaving them!

That made me feel funny, too, but it didn't

stop me. I crept around the porch and out the front gate.

All of the houses on our street were dark. It was so quiet that my footsteps echoed on the cobblestones and scared me.

Too quiet. I suddenly realized the band had stopped playing, which meant the show was beginning without me! I started to run. The sound of my feet clattering down the street set the neighborhood dogs to barking, but I ran faster and faster, until the huge tent loomed out of the darkness like a fantastic castle.

Strings of electric bulbs outlined the curve of the roof. Flags hanging from its center poles flapped softly. The sides of the tent were rolled all the way up to let the breeze in. In the dim light inside, hundreds of people were sitting on folding chairs.

Practically everyone in Cane County was crowded into that tent. Without even trying, I spotted Mr. and Mrs. Green, Charlie's folks; my piano teacher, Mrs. MacMurray;

the Larkins; Sheriff Barfield, his wife, and their redheaded twins; Mrs. Cormier, the elementary school principal; our preacher, Mr. Norwood. If even one of them caught sight of me, I'd be going to bed at seven o'clock for the rest of my life!

I edged closer anyway, squeezing between parked cars and buggies, until I could see part of the stage. It was a large wooden rectangle, raised off the ground on thick posts. Underneath it, a swarm of black electric fans whirred back and forth, pushing the warm air across huge blocks of ice to cool off the audience.

A bunch of little boys—Charlie Green was right in the middle of them—were sitting cross-legged on the ground in front of the fans. They were craning their necks to see what was happening onstage, directly above them.

The platform for the band was in my way, though. I'd have to circle around the tent to the other side if I wanted to see the show.

I crept past the empty ticket booth, stopping long enough to read the big cardboard sign: EAST LYNNE, A DRAMA IN TWO ACTS it announced in three-inch letters.

The names and photographs of all the actors were on the poster, too. Mr. West stared out at me from the top left corner, a twinkle in his eyes, his mustache bristling. The redheaded woman I'd seen that afternoon was Bertie West, his wife.

Further down the poster was a picture of the man who had given Frances his rosebud—George McIntyre—wearing the striped vest he'd had on that day. The young woman in the yellow silk dress was Gloria Garner.

There were smaller photographs of the other actors, dancers, and musicians, but I didn't waste any more time. I wanted to see the real thing.

Staying in the shadows, I darted past the door to the backstage stairs, and threaded my way through the cars parked on the far side of the tent. I crouched down behind an old Ford, raising up just far enough to see the stage over a front fender. Then I caught my breath!

One look at that stage, and I was carried thousands of miles from Caldwell, to a living room in England. There was a thick carpet on the floor, a fireplace glowing with electric flames, gold-framed paintings on the walls, and lots of fancy furniture. As hot as it was that evening, one of the men in the room had on striped wool trousers and a long black coat with two rows of gold buttons. The other one wore a tweed suit. The woman was dressed in a floor-length blue-green gown. On her head sat a large hat with a floppy brim and flowers around the crown.

If no one in the audience coughed or rattled a program, I could hear the actors. The woman was saying, "I'm afraid, Archibald! What if someone recognizes Richard and tells the police?"

"Richard has been away a long time," the man in the striped trousers answered. "Most people have forgotten all about him. There is a risk, but I don't see any other way . . . "

And Richard, in the tweeds, said, "Don't be afraid for me, Barbara. Anything is better than the life I'm living now. Think what it would mean to Mother if I could establish my innocence. . . . "

Sara spoke for the lady in a quick, nervous voice, for Archibald in a calm, kindly one. When she was Richard, she stammered a lit-

tle. Then she was Archibald again: "Make haste, Richard, and come back as soon as you can!"

Ellie closed her eyes, and it sounded like three completely different people were standing under the cypress. She opened her eyes when Sara stopped talking and peered down at her.

"What happened next?" Ellie asked. "Did the police get Richard?"

"No—next the villain appeared, a hateful man named Mr. Levison," Sara replied, shaking her head. "He turned Archibald's wife, Isabel, against her husband."

"Then what?" said Ellie, moving a little farther down the tree.

"Then the curtain dropped," Sara told her. "It was the end of Act One."

"Ellie? Ell-iee!" someone yelled from the front yard.

Ellie froze. "Carol Ann Kincannon!" she whispered to Sara. "*Sssh!* If we don't say anything, maybe she'll go away!"

Carol Ann Drops By

Ellie and Carol Ann Kincannon were the same age. They had known each other all their lives. There was no stopping Carol Ann—she liked to get to the bottom of things. When nobody answered her call, she simply charged around the house and into the backyard.

"I know you're out here! I heard those dogs barking!" she was muttering. Carol Ann hardly ever stopped talking. "Ellie Bremer! What are you doing up in that tree? Have you forgotten we're practically fourth graders?!"

Before Ellie could answer back, however,

Carol Ann had noticed Sara. For once, she hushed, looking up at Ellie and raising her eyebrows for an explanation.

"Oh. Uh—Carol Ann, this is Mrs. . . . Miss," Ellie fumbled.

"Sara Forster," Sara said from the white lawn chair. "How are you, Carol Ann?"

"Fine, thank you," Carol Ann replied, sizing up Sara before starting in on Ellie again. "Ellie, why are you in the tree?" she asked for the second time. She crossed her arms disapprovingly and waited for an answer.

Ellie sighed. "I didn't want to go to Mrs. Dowe's," she said at last.

"To try on your bridesmaid dress?" said Carol Ann. "Why ever not? I saw it the last time I was there. It's ab-so-lutely gorgeous!" Carol Ann talked that way when she wanted to sound older.

"I don't *need* the dress, because I'm . . . not . . . going . . . to . . . be . . . in . . . the . . . wedding!" Ellie said grimly, leaving lots of pauses after every word so there could be no misunderstanding.

"Don't be silly! Weddings are more fun than anything!" Carol Ann exclaimed. "I had the best time of my life at my cousin Nancy's."

She glanced over at Sara, who was leafing through her book. Then Carol Ann squinted up at Ellie again.

"Come on down," Carol Ann said. "It's roasting out here. Let's go to the drugstore and cool off with some lime freezes."

Ellie shook her head. "I'm not coming down, not for a month or so, if that's what it takes."

"Oh, yeah?" Carol Ann said. "And just how do you intend to sleep? And eat?"

"I'll tie myself to the tree," Ellie replied carelessly. "And I'll sneak down in the middle of the night and raid the kitchen when I'm hungry."

"You're acting like a baby!" Carol Ann said crossly. "Mary Beth's your sister, and you're going to be in that wedding whether you like it or not!"

"Gonna be kind of hard to be in the wedding if I'm up a tree," Ellie said, pressing her lips together.

"Never mind—I'll ask Dana Rogers to go to the drugstore with me!" Carol Ann said, scowling. "I'll see *you* when you grow up! Pleased to meet you," she murmured to Sara before walking stiffly across Ellie's backyard and disappearing around the house.

Sara put her book down and looked up at Ellie.

"Carol Ann gets mad when people don't do what she thinks they ought to," Ellie explained. Then she paused. That wasn't anything like her being upset with Mary Beth, was it?

Ellie wrinkled her nose, a little uncomfortable. She decided she'd think about *that* later—first she wanted to hear the end of Sara's story. "After the curtain dropped, did anybody see you?"

"No—the curtain was lowered, and the houselights came on just long enough for the band to take its place," Sara answered. "Then the musicians started playing a waltz.

"A tall man in a tuxedo and a woman wearing a black-and-white evening dress glided onto the stage. They swayed to the music, followed by a circle of bright blue light.

"Very few people in the audience had left

their seats—I thought it'd be safe to crawl out from behind the Ford and stretch my legs for a second. I'd just stood up when I saw her!"

"Saw who?" Ellie said, hanging out of the cypress by one arm.

"My sister, Frances!" said Sara. "And that's not all! She was kissing somebody!"

Sara Goes Backstage

I wouldn't have seen Frances at all if it hadn't been for the moon. It was almost full, floating in the sky above the courthouse roof. It shone brightly enough to outline two people lingering just outside the tent. The girl's smooth, blond hair—Frances's hair—gleamed in the moonlight. The white stripes on the man's vest stood out like fence pickets. I remembered who wore a vest like that: George McIntyre!

The two of them talked quietly for a moment. Then they moved closer together. The man bent his head slowly, and their faces touched.

It's Frances, and she's kissing! I wanted to yell. My sister's kissing George McIntyre, in his striped vest!

I mashed my hand down on my mouth to muffle the giggles. There's mud in your eye, Kyle Sperry!

I hunched over and scooted forward between some parked cars. I *had* to get closer! But by the time I straightened up again, I didn't see Frances and George anywhere!

Suddenly a square of light streamed out of the tent. The door to the backstage stairs had opened.

I'll bet he took Frances inside to show her around, I thought. What if I sneaked a peek? No, Frances might see me. . . . What if she does? I argued with myself. Maybe *I* slipped out of the house when I wasn't supposed to. But I'm not going around kissing actors, am I?!

I sidled up to the door—and forgot all about my sister. A short flight of steps led to a wooden platform crammed with boxes, scenery . . . and show people!

Actors and actresses, in costume and out, were practicing their lines, helping each other with makeup and wigs, laughing at jokes, flipping through magazines. Even picturing my father's sternest expression could not have kept me from dashing up those stairs, two at a time.

Nobody seemed to notice when I stepped onto the platform. No wonder—practically every inch of space was filled. Clothes spilled out of wardrobe trunks. Costumes hung from coatracks. A huge accordion was balanced on the bookkeeper's portable desk. Chairs and tables for the next act were stacked almost to the sloping ceiling.

The stage was on the other side of the canvas dressing rooms—the squawks of Mr. West's green parrot were drowned out by the waltz music. And the clicking of checkers on a trunk right next to me didn't register until someone spoke: "Why, hello there!"

I jumped a foot, and turned around to find two men smiling at me. One wore glasses and had graying hair. The other man was . . . Archibald, from the English living room!

He'd taken off his long black coat, but I recognized his striped trousers. His lips were red, his eyebrows thick and straight, his handlebar mustache a glossy brown.

He didn't look like anyone I knew, but there was something about his voice. . . .

Archibald spoke again. "How's your pretty sister?"

"Huh?" I said. Was he talking about Frances?

Archibald lifted up one side of the mustache so I could see his face. "George McIntyre," he said. "We met this afternoon, didn't we?"

I nodded, flabbergasted. George McIntyre, in a white shirt with no vest, and striped trousers, playing checkers. If he'd been in the tent the whole time, who had Frances been kissing?!

Before I could retreat down the stairs to

find out, a young woman burst out of the ladies' dressing room, dragging a little boy with her.

"Jim?" she called. "Where are you?"

Mr. West stepped out of the men's dressing room, squeezing into a jacket. "Yes, Gloria?" he said. The young woman was Gloria Garner, Isabel in Act One.

"Just look at him!" said Gloria, pointing to the boy. "He's got chicken pox!"

The boy grinned sheepishly. His face was covered with red spots.

"I was afraid he might catch them," Gloria went on. "In Dallas he played all afternoon with that child at the hotel, just before she came down with them."

"Looks like somebody poured red ants over his head," said an older actress with a long, thin nose. "No amount of makeup in the world could hide that."

"What are you talking about—makeup?" Gloria exclaimed indignantly. "He's going straight to bed!"

Mr. West threw his hands up in the air. "What next?" he groaned. "A tornado in Coopersville, a flash flood in San Antone, and now chicken pox in Caldwell." He thought for a minute. "Well, we haven't got any other kids. I guess we'd better change some lines real fast. It's almost time for the jugglers, and then we're on again with Act Two."

"Hang on, Boss," George McIntyre said. "What about this little lady?"

He meant me!

"It's a boy's part," said Gloria. "Although, at this age, I guess it doesn't make much difference." I had on overalls, after all—boys' clothes. There was a problem with my Buster Brown bowl haircut, though.

"She can wear a wig," George pointed out.

"What if the costume doesn't fit her?" said the older actress.

"It's just pajamas and a robe," said George. "Who's going to notice if they're a little too short? She'll be lying on the couch for most of the scene, anyway. You'll be dying," he explained to me.

"It might work," Mr. West said. "The last time we borrowed a kid was in . . ."

"I can't!" I interrupted. "I'm not supposed to be here at all! My folks will kill me!"

"You don't have to worry about that, honey," said Gloria. "After I get through with you, your own mother wouldn't know you."

"What about it?" George gave my shoulder a pat. "You'd sure be helping us out."

I was sorely tempted—what a story to tell my friends!

"Free passes for your whole family for the rest of the week," Mr. West offered.

My family couldn't use the passes, because I could never tell them about that night. Still—I couldn't resist.

"I'll do it!" I said.

On Stage

"Wow!" said Ellie. She was dangling from the next-to-the-lowest branch of the cypress. "Weren't you scared? I almost pass out at my piano recitals!"

Sara shook her head. "I'd been in some plays in school. I kind of enjoyed showing off."

"What did George McIntyre mean about you dying?" Ellie wanted to know.

"Well, people loved sad plays in those days, and *East Lynne* was one of the saddest. Richard is being chased by the police for something he didn't do. Archibald and Isabel's marriage breaks up. The evil Mr. Levison tells her that Archibald is really in love with someone else, and Isabel runs away.

"Then poor Isabel goes from riches to rags," Sara went on. "She returns to East Lynne to find her young son dying.

"That was my part—Isabel's son, Little Willie."

Gloria and Mr. West's wife, Bertie, took me into the ladies' dressing room and went to work. Bertie wrapped my hair flat with strips of cloth. Gloria explained my part while she put on my makeup.

"Your name is Willie," Gloria said, smearing my face with thick, white goop. "Isabel—that's me—is working for your father, Archibald, and his second wife, taking care of you. . . ."

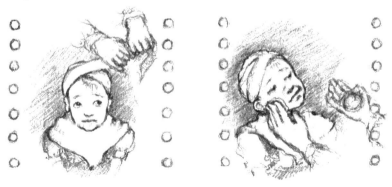

The dance music had stopped. The audience applauded loudly on the other side of the curtain, and the jugglers started their routine.

"You don't know it"—Gloria dotted rouge on my cheeks—"but Isabel is really your mama. She and your daddy were divorced so long ago that no one recognizes her now." Gloria spread the rouge around with her middle finger.

"She's real worried about you, because you're a very sick little boy. In fact, you're going to die at the end of the play." Gloria dipped a little brush into a bottle of brown liquid and painted tiny curved eyebrows on my forehead, above my own.

"It won't be anything fancy," Gloria continued. "You'll just say a few words, like,

'Where is Papa?' and 'I'm on my way to heaven—I heard the doctor tell Papa so the other day.' "

Gloria stuck another little brush into some melted mascara. "In a little while, Isabel keels over, too. Look up at the ceiling and hold still." She held my chin steady as she carefully brushed mascara onto my lashes.

"Bertie here'll go over your lines with you," Gloria finished, gathering up her pots and jars.

"I'll also whisper them to you onstage, just in case you forget something," Bertie said. "I'll be right there with you, playing a maid named Joyce."

I nodded cautiously—my face felt very stiff. Gloria and Bertie slipped a curly blond wig over my wrapped-up head, then helped

me into white pajamas and a maroon robe.

I glanced at myself in the mirror. Gloria was probably right—even my own mother wouldn't know me. Still, I was just as glad she was sitting in our living room eight blocks away, and not in the audience.

Act Two was beginning, with Archibald, Isabel, and the evil Mr. Levison on stage for the first scene. Bertie West and I went into a corner and practiced my lines, over and over.

Scene Three, the one I was in, came all too soon. The curtain thumped down, and Archibald and Mr. Levison rushed offstage. Bertie West and a half-numb Sara Forster rushed on.

I lay down on the couch, Bertie arranged some covers around me, and the curtain slowly rose.

I was *on stage*, with the whole county looking up at me. I gazed out at that audience, saw the warmth and concern in their faces for a sick little boy—and I never wanted it to end!

My long-lost mother, Isabel, started weeping and clutching me to her, saying she should never have doubted Archibald.

I said my lines just the way I was supposed to—pitiful, but not *too* pitiful: "Did you know my mama?" and "She was not quite good to Papa and me."

Out of the corner of my eye, I watched the audience, row after row of farmers in faded overalls, women in printed cotton dresses,

children, grandparents, all sniffling into their handkerchiefs. I felt so powerful! I could actually make people cry. I knew I could make them laugh, too. If only the play could go on and on . . .

Suddenly I heard a bump backstage. I glanced sideways in time to see Mr. West make a second grab for a large, curly brown dog, and miss—it was Snip!

Usually when Snip went for his nightly run, he'd chase one of the cottontails that lived in the willow thicket behind our house.

But that evening he'd come across the scent of much more interesting game at the bottom of the hackberry tree. He'd put his blood-hound nose to the ground and trailed me to the tent show, and nobody was going to stop him from tracking me down.

Talk about ruining a mood! Some of the audience spotted Snip as soon as he stepped onto the stage, and they began to chuckle. Head down, tail straight up, he zigzagged back and forth on the thick carpet, and the laughter grew.

"Go away!" Bertie West hissed under her breath. But Snip was on the trail, and I knew I was a goner.

Snip tracked me slowly across the stage to the couch. He sniffed at my feet wrapped in blankets, raised his nose in the air and gave a single, mournful bark. Then he jumped right on top of me, and started licking my face!

Over the roars of the crowd, I heard Charlie Green shout, "I know who that is up there! It's not Little Willie—it's Sara Forster!"

Taking Chances

"Oh, no!" Ellie giggled. She was draped across the lowest limb of the cypress on her stomach, her arms hanging down on one side, her legs on the other.

"Maybe my own mother wouldn't have known me, but my dog sure did." Sara chuckled. "Snip was heavy. I managed to shove him off me just in time to see my sister leap to her feet in the third or fourth row. Kyle stood up next to her. He was wearing a gray-and-white striped vest."

"It was just *Kyle* she was kissing?" Ellie said.

"Kyle, after all," Sara replied.

"What did you do then?" asked Ellie. "I would have wanted to drop through the stage, with everybody laughing at me."

"All those people had paid to see *East Lynne*," Sara said. "We had to finish the act. Mr. West dragged Snip away. We waited until the audience had calmed down a little, and we went on with our lines as best we could.

"I died, and Isabel died, then Archibald and his second wife said a few words. The curtain came down at last."

Sara leaned back in the lawn chair and fanned herself with her book again. "That's when the trouble *really* started. My parents had checked on me before they went to bed, and found my nightgown on a pillow instead of on me. And where would I be at nine thirty at night, if not at the tent show? They were waiting for me backstage."

Sara laughed, remembering. "I went to

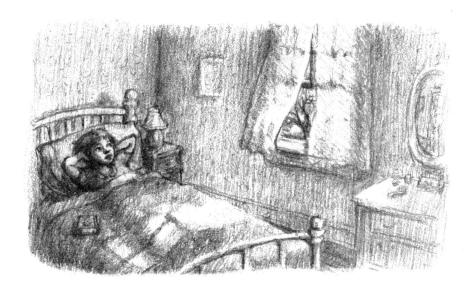

bed at seven o'clock all summer long. The sun would still be shining outside, I could hear the other kids out playing, and I'd be in bed, with the curtains drawn."

She patted Shorty. "I had lots to think about, though. My big night at the tent show, *before* Snip joined me on my deathbed. How the tent had looked, looming out of the darkness behind the courthouse! The way the stage makeup had smelled. How my stomach had felt just before the curtain went up. How I couldn't see anything at first, because of the bright lights. And then all of those faces, beaming at me."

Sara smiled at Ellie on the lowest limb. "From then on, I knew that's all I ever wanted to do." She shrugged. "And that's what I have done."

"You're an actress!" Ellie exclaimed. "Were you practicing your part before?"

"Right. I was rehearsing my lines in an English play I'm going to be in," Sara said, waving the book she was holding. "I'm not a movie actress," she went on to explain. "I wasn't pretty enough for that, goodness knows. Besides, I need to see that audience out there."

"What happened to your sister?" said Ellie.

"She still lives in Dillard," Sara said. "I'm down here visiting her."

"Did she and Kyle get married?" Ellie asked.

"No, Frances married a man with a dairy farm. They had five children. That's what

Frances always wanted—a big family." Sara threw her head back to gaze up at the milky-blue sky. "That's the important thing, I think. Knowing what you want to do. And maybe taking a few chances." She glanced at Ellie. "Mary Beth is taking a chance on a life with Mike. You'll be taking your own chances, Ellie."

"I could never be an actress," Ellie murmured.

"You don't have to be an actress," Sara told her. "That's the chance *I* took. Things happen, people come into your life, you learn from them. Anything is possible."

Maybe that's true, Ellie thought. If a little girl from Caldwell could grow up to be an actress . . . maybe I'll grow up to be a writer myself!

Suddenly Shorty raised his head and barked two short barks, which meant someone was coming. Ellie heard the rattle of her grandmother's car as it braked at the curb out front.

"They're back," Ellie said to Sara.

Sara nodded and got to her feet. "I'd better go in and see what Catherine's up to."

Ellie hugged the lowest limb of the cypress, swung under it, and hung for a moment. Then she dropped to the ground with a thud. "Hold on—I'm coming with you," Ellie said.